A Parents Magazine
Read Aloud Original

Travels with Tess and Tim

by Marc Gave
pictures by Abby Carter

PARENTS MAGAZINE PRESS
NEW YORK

for Lucy
M.G.

for Sarah Marie
A.C.

Text copyright © 1990 by Marc Gave.
Illustrations copyright © 1990 by Abby Carter.
Printed in the United States of America.
10 9 8 7 6 5 4 3 2 1

Library of Congress Cataloging in Publication Data

Gave, Marc.
Travels with Tess and Tim; pictures by Abby Carter
p.   cm.

Summary: Tess and Tim attend their cousin's
wedding with amusing results.
ISBN 0-8193-1192-8
[1. Brothers and sisters—Ficton. Weddings—Fiction.]
I. Carter, Abby, ill.   II. Title.
PZ7.G235Tf   1989
[E]—dc20   89-16401
                                        CIP
                                        AC

It was Saturday. It was summer.
But Tess woke up early anyway.

Then she came and woke me up.
We tiptoed to Mommy's
and Daddy's room.
We didn't hear anything.

"Good morning!" I said.
"It's almost six-thirty!" Tess said.
"We have to get going."

"Ohhh," Daddy sighed, sitting
on the edge of the bed.
"Ah me," Mommy said, yawning.

"Come on!" said Tess. "We have to go to Cousin Sarah's wedding."
"It only takes two hours to get there," Mommy answered.

I flew down the stairs.
"We should go by plane,"
I said. "Planes are fast."

"Tim's right," Tess said.
"Cars are slow.
And Mrs. Wiggles and I
won't have anything to do."

"Eat your breakfast," Daddy said,
"or we'll never get there at all."
Tess was already feeding
Mrs. Wiggles.

After breakfast Cathy came over.
She lives next door.
"Here's the key," Mommy said.

"Good-bye, and thanks for taking care
of Puss and Boots while we're away."

We rode a few blocks.
Dr. Pine waved at us.

Then Tess started to be a pest.
"I'm hungry," she said.
"We just ate," Mommy answered.
"Aren't we there yet?" Tess whined.

I was glad when she snuggled up
with Mrs. Wiggles and went to sleep.

"Wake up, Tess," I said. "We're here."
Tess opened one eye.
"Where?" she asked.

"At the hotel."
"Where's Cousin Sarah?" said Tess.
"At her house, getting ready for tomorrow."
"What's tomorrow?" Tess asked.

"Are you still asleep?" I said.
"Tomorrow is Cousin Sarah's wedding."
"Oh, I remember," Tess answered.
"I'm the flower girl,
and you're going to carry the ring."

We went up to our hotel room.
I bounced on the bed.
Tess opened
the drawers.

The glasses in the bathroom
were wrapped in paper.
So were the little soaps.
So was the toilet seat.

"I'm hungry," said Tess.
Mommy picked up the phone.
"I'll tell Aunt Betty we're here,"
she said. "Then we'll drive over
to her house for lunch."

Aunt Betty opened the door.
"Hi, everybody!" she said. "Come on in."
Cousin Sarah showed us her wedding dress.
Tess showed Mrs. Wiggles to Cousin Sarah.

We all helped ourselves to lunch.
Tess dropped hers in the iced tea.

Then I played with the dog.
Tess spent the whole time
following Cousin Sarah around.

"We have to go back to the hotel now,"
Daddy said. "It's time to get ready
for the wedding rehearsal
and the rehearsal dinner."

The rehearsal dinner?
I couldn't figure out
why we had to practice eating.

THE WEDDING

"Just remember what you did at the rehearsal last night," Mommy said. "But this time Tess will have flowers in her basket instead of Mrs. Wiggles."

"I'm taking Mrs. Wiggles, too," said Tess.
Mommy shook her head. "You can't carry
the basket *and* Mrs. Wiggles *and* throw
flowers all at the same time."

Tess wouldn't give up.
"*Tim* can carry the flowers,"
she said. "I'll hold the ring.
Then I can carry Mrs. Wiggles, too."

Tess started crying when Mommy said
she had to be the flower girl.
"Why can't Tim do it?" she begged.

Uncle Dave
came in.

Mommy told him why Tess was crying.
"There's no time to figure this out,"
said Uncle Dave.
"The music
is starting!"

That's how I became the first
flower boy in history.
I wasn't too happy about it.

After the wedding we stood in line
with Cousin Sarah and her new husband.
Everyone hugged and kissed.

Cousin Sarah talked to me
at the wedding reception.
She said, "I will always
remember how you saved the day
by being flower boy."

She thanked me with a big kiss.
I felt very proud.

About the Author

Marc Gave is a children's book editor and also loves to read. When he is looking for a new story idea, he has to pull himself away from reading and editing. "You can never tell when a good idea will come along," Mr. Gave says. "You have to be there to notice it as the idea passes by."

Mr. Gave lives in New York with his wife and two children. This is his second *Tess and Tim* book.

About the Artist

Like Tess and Tim, *Abby Carter* recently went travelling. With her husband, Doug, she moved from Long Island, outside of New York City, to live in Maine, in a house that overlooks the sea. Ms. Carter grew up in Maine—with *three* brothers instead of one.

Abby Carter also illustrated the first *Tess and Tim* book published by Parents.